Karen's School Surprise

**Look for these
and other books about Karen
in the
Baby-sitters Little Sister series:**

Little Sister

Karen's School Surprise
Ann M. Martin

Illustrations by Susan Tang

A
LITTLE APPLE
PAPERBACK

SCHOLASTIC INC.
New York Toronto London Auckland Sydney

No part of this publication may be reproduced in whole or in part, or stored in a retrieval system, or transmitted in any form or by any means, electronic, mechanical, photocopying, recording, or otherwise, without written permission of the publisher. For information regarding permission, write to Scholastic Inc., 555 Broadway, New York, NY 10012.

ISBN 0-590-69185-6

12 11 10 9 8 7 6 5 4 3 2 1   6 7 8 9/9 0 1/0

Printed in the U.S.A.   40

First Scholastic printing, September 1996

The author gratefully acknowledges
Stephanie Calmenson
for her help
with this book.

Karen's School Surprise

Saturday Morning at the Big House

Ring, ring! It was Saturday morning at the big house. Kristy, my big sister, answered the phone. (It was for her.)

Ding-dong! Elizabeth, my stepmother, answered the doorbell. (It was the mailman, with a package.)

Whirr, whirr! Daddy was running the leaf blower in the backyard. (There were autumn leaves everywhere.)

The big house is always exciting. And noisy. I love it!

My name is Karen Brewer. I am seven

1

years old. I have blonde hair, blue eyes, and a bunch of freckles. I also have a lot of brothers and sisters.

"Karen, do you want to make Play-Doh monsters with me?" asked Andrew.

Andrew is my little brother. He is four going on five.

"Karen read Emmie story," said Emily.

Emily is my little sister. She is two and a half.

Then Nannie came out of the kitchen. Nannie is my stepgrandmother.

"Karen, did you say you wanted to bake cookies with me today? I'm ready whenever you are," she said.

I am a very popular person.

"Sorry, everyone. I already have plans with Hannie," I explained.

Hannie Papadakis is one of my two best friends. She lives across the street and one house over from the big house.

"See you later!" called David Michael. He whizzed past us and headed for the door.

David Michael is seven, like me. He was

on his way to meet Linny, Hannie's older brother.

"I will see you over there," I said. I ran upstairs to get my sweater, then headed out the door.

Honk, honk!

Sam and Charlie, my older brothers, waved. They were pulling up in Charlie's old car, the junk bucket. I waved back, then looked both ways and crossed the street. David Michael was heading back in my direction.

"What's going on?" I asked.

"Hannie and Linny forgot they were going to visit their grandparents this morning," replied David Michael.

Hannie came running toward me.

"I am really sorry, Karen," she said. "I will call you when I get home, okay?"

"No problem," I replied.

David Michael and I walked back to the house together. Andrew and Emily were settled in the den watching *School Stars* on TV. *School Stars* is a really cool show.

Classes of school kids get to go on TV to answer questions and do goofy things. I have seen kids run through Jell-O. Now some kids were having a relay race while they wore hats with raw eggs on top.

"Ew! Ew! The egg is dripping down his nose!" said Andrew.

Emily was giggling.

"For two points, where in Florida is the space flight launching center?" asked Mr. Stevens, the show's host.

"Cape Canaveral!" I shouted.

"Orlando!" said David Michael.

One of the contestants answered Cape Canaveral.

"That is correct!" said Mr. Stevens.

"Yeah! I got it right!" I cried, jumping up and down.

"Now for three points, how many esses are in Mississippi?"

I spelled it out to myself.

"Four!" I shouted. I even beat the contestants.

"Three?" said David Michael.

"The correct answer is four. M-I-S-S-I-S-S-I-P-P-I," spelled Mr. Stevens.

By the end of the show I had gotten only three answers wrong. David Michael had gotten only three answers right. Oh, well. Not everyone can be as good at *School Stars* as me!

Big and Little

I bet you already think I have a big family, but you have not even met everyone yet! You see, I have *two* families — a big family and a little family. And I have two houses — a big house and a little house. This is how it happened.

A long time ago, when I was still in preschool, I lived in one big house with Mommy, Daddy, and Andrew. Then Mommy and Daddy started fighting a lot. They explained to Andrew and me that they loved us very much, but they did not

7

want to live with each other anymore. That was when they got a divorce.

Mommy moved with Andrew and me to a little house not too far away from the big house in Stoneybrook, Connecticut. Daddy stayed at the big house. (It is the house he grew up in.)

Then Mommy and Daddy each got married again. Mommy married a man named Seth. Now he is my stepfather. Daddy married Elizabeth. Now she is my stepmother. And Andrew and I live at both houses — a month at the big house, a month at the little house. Back and forth.

So these are the people who live at the little house: Mommy, Seth, Andrew, and me. We also have pets. They are Midgie, who is Seth's dog; Rocky, who is Seth's cat; Emily Junior, who is my pet rat (I named her after my little sister); and Bob, who is Andrew's hermit crab.

You already met everyone at the big house, but in case you forgot who they are I will tell you. They are Daddy and Elizabeth and Elizabeth's four children from her first marriage: David Michael; Kristy, who is thirteen and the best stepsister ever; and Sam and Charlie, who are so old they are in high school.

I have one other sister, Emily Michelle. Daddy and Elizabeth adopted her from a faraway country called Vietnam.

I also have a wonderful stepgrandmother. Nannie is Elizabeth's mother.. She came to live with us to help take care of Emily. Now she helps take care of everyone and we do not know what we would do without her.

The pets who live at the big house are Shannon, David Michael's big Bernese mountain dog puppy; Boo-Boo, Daddy's cranky old cat; Crystal Light the Second, my goldfish; and Goldfishie, Andrew's you-know-what. Emily Junior and Bob live at the big house whenever Andrew and I are there.

Guess what. I gave Andrew and me special names. I call us Andrew Two-Two and

Karen Two-Two. (I got that name from a book my teacher read to our class. It was called *Jacob Two-Two Meets the Hooded Fang*.)

I gave us those names because we have two of so many things. We have two mommies and two daddies, two cats and two dogs, two families and two houses. We each have two sets of clothes and toys and books — one set at each house. I have two bicycles. Andrew has two tricycles. I have two stuffed cats. Goosie lives at the little house and Moosie lives at the big house. And I have my two best friends. Hannie lives across the street from the big house and Nancy Dawes lives next door to the little house. We are in the same second-grade class at Stoneybrook Academy and we like to do everything together. That is why we call ourselves the Three Musketeers.

Sometimes being a two-two is confusing. But mostly it is fine. I like it. I am very lucky to have two families who love me.

The Coolest
Announcement

It was Monday morning. Our teacher, Ms. Colman, had not come in yet. Hannie and Nancy and I were at the back of our classroom talking. I used to sit at the back of the room with them. Then I got my glasses and Ms. Colman moved me up front. She said I could see better from there. And you know what? She was right.

My friends and I were pretending we were hosting an awards ceremony. We took turns announcing the new arrivals.

"And here comes Pamela Harding with

11

her good friends Jannie Gilbert and Leslie Morris!" I said. "They are wearing matching denim skirts today."

Pamela is my best enemy. Jannie and Leslie are her two best friends.

"Here come Ricky Torres and his buddy Bobby Gianneli," said Hannie. "Ricky, as your viewers may know, is Karen's pretend husband."

This is true. Ricky and I got married on the playground one day.

"And now let's hear it for the Barkan twins, Terri and Tammy!" said Nancy.

The kids started pouring in. Addie Sidney rolled into class in her wheelchair. Natalie Springer stopped to pull up her droopy socks and almost tripped Audrey Green who was right behind her. Hank Reubens and Omar Harris were tossing a softball back and forth on the way in. Sara Ford dropped her notebook and Chris Lamar picked it up for her.

"Wait!" I said into a make-believe microphone. "Here comes our special host, Ms. Colman!"

The Three Musketeers started clapping when Ms. Colman walked in.

"Thank you very much, girls," she said, smiling. "Now if everyone will settle down we can get started."

Ms. Colman chose Hannie to take attendance. I wish she had chosen me. I like doing important jobs. But since Hannie is a Musketeer I did not mind too much.

When she finished, Ms. Colman said seven of my favorite words. (I counted them once.) She said, "Class, I have an announcement to make."

"Yes!" I called out. That is because I could tell it was going to be a Surprising Announcement.

Ms. Colman gave me her you-forgot-to-use-your-indoor-voice look. I know that look very well because I get excited and forget a lot.

"Sorry," I said.

Ms. Colman smiled. (Did I tell you that Ms. Colman is a gigundoly wonderful teacher? Well, she is.)

"How many of you know the TV show *School Stars*?" she asked.

Everyone's hand shot up.

"I thought so," said Ms. Colman. "Well, I found out yesterday that our class might be able to be on the show."

"Ye — !" I started to call out. But I covered my mouth instead.

"Each class that would like to be on the show must take a quiz to qualify. The classes that score the highest will get to be on the show. And if we get to be on the show, we could win a weekend trip to Camp Outer Space. If you would like for us to take the quiz, please raise your hand."

Every hand in the room shot up. I was so excited I was bouncing up and down in my seat.

"Well, I guess it is unanimous then," said Ms. Colman. "I will contact the show and get the quiz for you to take as soon as possible."

I turned and gave Hannie and Nancy the thumbs-up sign. This was one of the coolest Surprising Announcements ever!

Grumpy

Nancy's mother dropped her off at the big house after school. The Three Musketeers had decided to start practicing goofy stunts in case we got to be on the show.

"I will be right back!" I called.

We were in the big-house backyard. I ran into the kitchen and came out with three plastic bowls and three plastic cups.

"Here's what we are going to do," I said. "We each have to take a bowl and put it on our heads like this."

I put a bowl on my head right-side up.

"Then we put a cup into the bowl like this," I said.

I put a cup into the bowl upside down.

"I know," said Nancy. "We have to hop around that tree three times with the bowl and cup on our heads."

"And if we drop anything we have to start over," said Hannie.

"Get your bowls and cups ready," I called. "One, two, three, go!"

We hopped halfway around the tree with the bowls and cups on our heads. Then we started laughing so hard that everything came tumbling down.

We tried again. We knew we could not start giggling on *School Stars*.

It took about ten tries, but each of us finally made it around the tree without dropping anything.

We tried a few more silly stunts after that. We made a leaf trail on the sidewalk and had to walk it like a tightrope.

Then we took turns trying to recite the Pledge of Allegiance with a mouthful of crackers.

Then it was time for Hannie and Nancy to go home.

I ran into the house. I had already told Nannie and Emily and Daddy about the show. I was happy when David Michael walked in so I could tell him, too. I wanted everyone to know.

Only David Michael was not so happy with my news. In fact, he was downright grumpy about it.

"You always get to do *everything*," he said. He went through the list of things I have done and he has not. I knew his list by heart.

"And you are always winning things, and now you get to go on another cool class trip!" he shouted.

I remembered the last time David Michael got mad at me like this. It was when my class got to go to the Museum of Natural History in New York to see the dinosaurs.

18

He was in a very bad mood then. He was failing tests in school and he said he hated his teacher.

"You do not have to shout at me," I said. "It is not my fault."

David Michael stormed off to his room. A few minutes later, Elizabeth came home from work. I told her my news. I figured she would be happy for me and she was.

"That is wonderful, Karen!" she said.

"I think so, too," I said. "But when I told David Michael about it he got grumpy."

"I will talk to him and see what's up," said Elizabeth.

She started to go upstairs to David Michael's room. But he was already coming down.

I did not want to be in the same room with my grumpy brother, so I went into the den.

"Hi, David Michael," said Elizabeth. "How was school?"

"Here's how," replied David Michael.

I peeked out and saw him hand his

mother a piece of paper. "I failed my math test. You need to sign it so I can take it back to school tomorrow."

So that was it. David Michael was grumpy because he had failed another test. Hmm. If I were failing tests all the time, I would be grumpy, too.

The Quiz

Hannie, Nancy, and I practiced doing silly stunts and watched *School Stars* together whenever we could.

Then on a Monday, exactly two weeks after Ms. Colman had made her Surprising Announcement, she came in waving a stack of papers. She had a big smile on her face.

"I have the quizzes from *School Stars*!" she said.

"Excellent!" I cried.

Oops. I forgot to use my indoor voice again. But this time I was not the only one.

My whole class forgot. We all shouted out loud.

"I know this is exciting, everyone. But the sooner you settle down, the sooner I can tell you about the quiz," said Ms. Colman.

She explained that each class that participated would be judged on its performance as a whole. If our class scored high enough, we would be entered into a drawing that would take place soon.

"And if your class entry is drawn, you will get to compete against another second-grade class on *School Stars*," said Ms. Colman.

To save time, Ms. Colman took attendance herself.

After she put away the attendance book, she handed out the quiz booklets.

"You are on your own now," said Ms. Colman. "I am not allowed to help you. You may open your booklets and begin as soon as I tell you."

"Wait, please!" I said. "I need to sharpen my pencil."

I sharpened my pencil. A few other kids sharpened theirs, too. Then we sat down again.

"Is everyone ready?" asked Ms. Colman.

"Wait, please!" I said. "I need to clean my glasses."

I took off my glasses and wiped them with my T-shirt. Then I put them back on.

"Is everyone ready?" asked Ms. Colman, looking at me.

"Ready," I replied.

"You may open your booklets," Ms. Colman said.

The quiz started out with spelling. This was a very good thing for me because I am an excellent speller. I even won a state spelling contest once.

Each word was spelled three different ways. We were supposed to circle the correct spelling. Here are a few of the spelling words I circled: *radiant, separate, lightly, com-*

pletely. I checked the words carefully, then went on to the math section.

There was some easy multiplication and division. The only problem I had trouble with was dividing thirty-six by four. To get the answer I drew thirty-six lines on the back of the booklet. Then I circled each group of four lines. When I counted the groups I got the answer. It was nine. (It is a good thing I am a fast speller. Drawing all those lines and counting the groups took a long time.)

I answered some easy geography and science questions next. Then I turned the page. There were no more questions. In the middle of the page it said, "Thank you for completing the *School Stars* quiz."

"You are welcome," I whispered. Then I closed my booklet.

After the quiz, Ms. Colman asked how we thought we had done. The class was very excited. We thought we had done very well.

"I am glad you feel good about the quiz," said Ms. Colman. "Just be careful about getting your hopes up. Remember that many other classes are taking the quiz, too."

I was not worried. I was sure my classmates and I had done well.

"*School Stars,* here we come!" I said to myself.

Look Who's Happy Now

A few days later, David Michael burst into the house after school.

"Hi, everyone!" he called. "Guess what! My class got a computer. It is a brand-new super-duper, do-everything computer! Now every class in my school has one."

David Michael was the happiest any of us had seen him in weeks.

Hmm. I wished my school had a new computer in every class. We have three computers in one room called the Computer Lab. We have to take turns using them.

"This is great news!" said Daddy. "Why don't you come into my office after dinner? We can look at some things on the computer I use."

Daddy used to go to work at an office, but now he works at home. He loves his computer. He says if it were not for his computer he could not work at home.

"What about our other computer?" I asked.

We have a second computer in our house. It is our family computer.

"That one is not half as good as the one in my office, Karen," said Daddy.

"Oh, I see," I replied.

Hmm. Getting a brand-new computer in his classroom was one thing. Getting special treatment from Daddy was another.

After dinner, Daddy took David Michael into his office. They did not come out for a long time. When they did, Daddy had his arm around David Michael.

"You can use my computer whenever I am not using it," said Daddy.

"Thanks!" replied David Michael. You should have seen his face. He was beaming.

"I will try to pick up some software that will help you with your schoolwork, too," continued Daddy.

David Michael and Daddy sure were having fun. I sat in the den kicking my feet against the bottom of the couch. There was a show on TV, but I had not heard a word of it. I was too busy listening to "The David Michael and Daddy Show."

The next thing I heard was David Michael asking if they could get CD-ROM for the computer.

"Sure," Daddy replied. "That's a terrific idea. I've been wanting to get into CD-ROM myself for some time. We can learn about it together."

What about me? David Michael's new computer at school was turning into a big deal. I did not like it one bit.

Heading for the Moon

After school on Thursday, Nancy and I went to Hannie's house to practice some more silly stunts.

When I got home, the door to Daddy's office was closed.

Knock, knock. I decided I wanted to tell Daddy about my day. I also wanted to see if David Michael was in there with him. Daddy opened the door.

"Hi, honey, what's up?" he said.

Sure enough, David Michael was sitting at Daddy's desk in front of his computer.

"Nothing important," I replied.

"I am just helping David Michael with his homework assignment," said Daddy. "We will be finished here in a couple of minutes."

I did not feel like telling Daddy about my stunts anymore. I went upstairs to tell Moosie about them instead. But he did not look very interested.

David Michael worked at Daddy's computer again after dinner. He was there the next night. And the next. And the next. It looked to me as though he were in Daddy's office more than out of it.

On Monday, David Michael came running into the house after school.

"I passed my math test!" he shouted. "I even got a high grade!"

"That is terrific!" said Nannie, hugging him.

Then Daddy stepped out of his office.

"I am very proud of you, David Michael," he said. "Come, look. I have a new program I want you to try out."

David Michael was getting really good at working with the computer. He and Daddy talked about it all the time at dinner. I could hardly understand them anymore.

I knew Daddy would teach me about the computer if I wanted to learn. But I did not have time now. I was too busy getting ready to appear with my class on *School Stars*. It was going to be so much fun.

But what if we did not qualify? Then I would not know about computers *and* I would not get to be on *School Stars*, either.

On Tuesday, I asked Ms. Colman as soon as she walked in, "Have you heard from *School Stars* yet?"

"I am afraid not, Karen," she replied. "I will let you know as soon as I do."

I asked her the same question on Wednesday and again on Thursday. The answer was the same.

On Friday, Ms. Colman came in with a big smile on her face.

"You heard from them! You heard!" I cried.

As soon as everyone was seated, Ms. Colman told us the news.

"I got a letter from the producers of *School Stars* yesterday afternoon. You have qualified for the drawing!" said Ms. Colman. "It will take place next week. Remember, if you get to be on the show, you could win a weekend at Camp Outer Space."

"Yea!" I shouted. "We qualified." I hoped that we got to be on the show. Camp Outer Space sounded gigundoly fun. I wiggled with excitement. I started jumping up and down. I looked around. My whole class was jumping up and down, too.

"Okay, kids. Settle down," said Ms. Colman. But she was smiling.

I stopped jumping and sat down in my seat. I did not call out anymore either.

Instead I had an exciting daydream. I dreamed I was captain of a spaceship. I floated around the cabin giving orders.

"Now hear this," I said to my crew. "We are heading for the moon!"

Nature Quiz

The following Friday, Ms. Colman walked into class with an even bigger smile on her face than before.

"Class, please be seated," she said.

I hurried to my seat. I zipped up my lips and clasped my hands in front of me.

"I received another letter yesterday from the *School Stars* producers," said Ms. Colman. "The drawing took place on Monday. You have been selected to appear on the show."

My classmates and I cheered.

As soon as the class settled down again, Ms. Colman told us the details.

"The show will be taped next week," she said. "You will have a much better chance of winning if you are prepared. That means you will have to be ready for both the quiz and the stunts. This morning, we will work as usual. Then, in the afternoon, we will begin preparing for the quiz."

The morning went by quickly. At recess, all anyone could talk about was the show. When we returned to our classroom in the afternoon, Ms. Colman divided us into groups and handed out quiz cards. Each group had a different subject. We took turns quizzing each other.

I was in a group with Ricky, Natalie, and Addie because we all sit up front together. (Ricky and Natalie are glasses wearers, like me. Addie sits up front because there is more room for her wheelchair there.)

Our subject was nature and I got to ask the first question. I picked up a quiz card and read, "True or false: There is no such thing as a striped dog."

We all answered false. I turned over the card. Guess what. We were wrong. The answer is true. There is no such thing as a striped dog.

It was Addie's turn to ask the next question.

"This is a two-part question. Here is the first part," she said. "What do you call a group of geese on the ground?"

"A gaggle!" I replied.

The other kids in my group thought I was right, so Addie turned over the card.

"Very good, Karen. A gaggle of geese is correct," she said, trying to sound like Ms. Colman. "Here is the second part of the question. What do you call a group of geese in the air?"

"A flying gaggle?" said Ricky.

"A giggle?" said Natalie.

"A jumbo jet with feathers?" I said.

"Very funny," said Addie. She turned

over the card and read, "A group of geese in the air is called a skein."

I closed my eyes and tried to memorize the word *skein* just in case they asked me on TV.

We learned a lot of interesting nature facts from our quiz. We learned that the farther apart footprints are, the faster a creature is running. We learned that African elephants are bigger than Indian elephants. And we learned that squirrels sometimes wrap themselves up in their bushy tails to keep warm.

Nature is a gigundoly interesting subject.

Stoneybrook Stunt Gym

On Monday morning, we were lining up for gym class when Ms. Colman said, "You will not be playing basketball or dodgeball this morning. Your gym activities today are going to be a surprise."

We marched down the hall as fast as we could. Our gym teacher, Mrs. Mackey, greeted us wearing a red clown nose. She squeezed the nose and we all started laughing.

"Welcome to the Stoneybrook Stunt Gym," she said. "It is my job to prepare you for the *School Stars* stunts. Is everybody ready?"

"Ready!" we replied.

"Everyone please take off your socks and sneakers and pile them up near the wall over here," said Mrs. Mackey. "Now, I would like you to make two lines facing each other. Karen, please stand over here. Ricky, you stand opposite Karen. Hannie stand next to Karen. Nancy stand next to Ricky."

When we were in two lines, Mrs. Mackey held up a balloon. "This stunt is called 'Balloon Bash,' " she said. "The idea is to step on the balloon and bash it. Whoever breaks it is the winner."

She tossed the balloon down the aisle between us.

Everyone stomped on it as it passed by, but it did not break. It just kept slipping by us.

Stomp. Stomp-stomp! Stomp. Stomp-stomp!

"Keep trying," said Mrs. Mackey. She sent the balloon back down the aisle again.

Stomp. Stomp-stomp!

The balloon was almost in front of me.

Stomp. Stomp-stomp . . . whoosh!

I did it! I bashed the balloon! Water sprayed all over the place.

"Good job, Karen!" said Mrs. Mackey.

We bashed two more water balloons. Addie rolled over one with her wheelchair. Ricky broke the other with his foot.

Then we practiced some more stunts. We had wheelbarrow races. Hannie held my ankles while I ran across the gym on my hands. We were the fastest in the class.

We had a Ping-Pong ball and spoon race. You had to put a Ping-Pong ball in a spoon, then race to the other side of the gym. Pamela and Bobby tied in that race.

Finally, Mrs. Mackey told us that gym class was over. Boo. The Stoneybrook Stunt Gym was so much fun, I wished it could have lasted all day long.

Computer Pals

When I got home from school, the door to Daddy's office was closed. I figured David Michael was in there again.

I was wrong. David Michael was in the kitchen with Nannie and Emily, having an afternoon snack. (Andrew was not there because he had a play date.)

"Hi, everyone," I said.

"Come join us," said Nannie. "David Michael was just telling us about his new computer pal at school."

David Michael looked very excited.

"Everyone in my class was matched up with a computer pal," he said. "It's like a pen pal only you get to communicate on computers instead of the old-fashioned way. My computer pal is Mark. He lives in Oklahoma."

A computer pal sounded like fun. But I did not think David Michael had to act like such a big shot about it.

"My pen pal, Maxie, and I write to each other. We send presents, too. And Maxie is right in New York City, so we can visit each other. You cannot send presents or visit over a computer, you know."

"So what?" said David Michael. "Talking on a computer is cool."

Nannie turned to me.

"How was your day at school?" she asked.

"It was okay," I said.

I did not feel like talking about stunt class just then. I was too busy thinking about David Michael's computer pal.

"May I be excused, please? I want to try

talking to Mark on the computer," said David Michael. "I have two numbers for him. I think one is for his computer at home."

"Go right ahead," said Nannie. "I hope you are able to reach him."

"You cannot use Daddy's computer," I said. "His door is closed. That means he does not want to be disturbed."

"I will use our other computer," said David Michael.

He jumped up and headed for the den.

"May I be excused, too?" I asked.

"Of course," replied Nannie. "But you have not eaten much of your snack. Would you like something else?"

"No, thanks. I am just not very hungry," I said.

I followed David Michael into the den.

"Can I use the computer first?" I asked. "I want to play a game of Solitaire before I do my homework."

"I am busy now, Karen," said David Michael, pressing some keys on the keyboard.

"I told you I want to reach my pen pal at home. If I can do it, we will be able to talk to each other at school during the day and at home, too."

"Can't you call him later? You are hogging the computer," I replied.

The computer started making funny noises then. Then it sounded like a telephone dialing a number.

The screen flashed a message that said, *"You are now on-line. Please instruct."*

David Michael hit a few more keys. The screen went blank. He typed in, "Hello, Mark. This is David Michael. Are you there?"

Below his message a new message appeared. It said, "I am here! What's happenin', dude?"

"I did it!" David Michael shouted. "I am having a conversation with Mark in Oklahoma!"

"Big deal," I said, even though I was impressed. "All I know is that you are hogging the computer."

I hung around and waited while David Michael and Mark chatted on-line. They told each other their ages, where they lived, and what sports they enjoyed. It looked like so much fun. I wished I could talk to Maxie on the computer. I didn't know if she had one at home. Even if she did, I would not know how to reach her.

I went upstairs to do my homework. I did not really want to play Solitaire anyway.

Shaving Cream

At school on Monday, Ms. Colman made another Surprising Announcement.

"Mr. Berger's class is not in the drawing for *School Stars*. But they have been taking quizzes and practicing stunts just for fun," she said. "Mr. Berger and I arranged a mock *School Stars* show for our two classes this afternoon."

Mr. Berger teaches the second-grade class next door. Our classes met in the gym after lunch. Mrs. Mackey was getting ready for our stunts. Instead of her clown nose, she was wearing a shiny black top hat.

"Good afternoon, contestants! I am your show host today," she said in a fancy announcer's voice. "Now, please take your seats. Ms. Colman's class on the red line. Mr. Berger's class on the blue."

We sat down on the colored lines taped to the gym floor.

"And now I will call up our first contestants," said Mrs. Mackey. "We will start with Karen Brewer from Ms. Colman's class and Liddie Yuan from Mr. Berger's class. Please stand behind the desk over there."

At one end of the gym was a desk. On top of the desk was a bell.

"I will ask a question," said Mrs. Mackey. "If you think you know the answer, ring the bell and wait for me to call on you. If you answer correctly, you score three points. If you miss, your opponent has a chance to answer the same question. If your opponent does not answer correctly, it will be time for a silly stunt."

I hoped we did not get *all* the answers

right. A silly stunt would be fun.

"Listen carefully to the first question," said Mrs. Mackey. "For three points, please tell me which elephant is larger — the African or the Indian."

I was first to ring the bell.

"Karen, your answer, please," said Mrs. Mackey.

"That is easy. The African elephant!" I replied.

My classmates cheered.

"Good for you! That gives Ms. Colman's class three points," said Mrs. Mackey. "Here is the second question, also for three points. Why do catfish have whiskers?"

Ding, ding! I was the first to ring the bell again. But as soon as Mrs. Mackey said my name, I realized I did not know the answer.

"Um, let me see. Is it because they forgot to shave?" I said.

Everybody laughed.

"I am afraid not," said Mrs. Mackey. "Liddie, can you answer that question for us?"

"Because they are part of the cat family?" said Liddie.

"That is also incorrect," said Mrs. Mackey.

"Stunt! Stunt!" shouted our classmates.

This is what Liddie and I had to do. We each had to run through a maze drawn in colored chalk on the gym floor. Every time one of us stepped on a line, we would be squirted with shaving cream by the kids in our class.

By the end I was covered with shaving cream. But I finished first and scored two points.

The afternoon went by in a flash. By the end, our class was ahead six points. We had won our very first *School Stars* competition. This seemed to me like a good sign.

Please Go
to Your Rooms

I burst into the big house after school.

"My class won *School Stars*!" I cried.

"You were on *School Stars*?" said Nannie. "And you did not tell us?"

"It was not the real show. It was a pretend show we had in gym today with Mr. Berger's class," I replied.

I told Nannie, Andrew, and Emily about the questions and stunts.

Then David Michael burst into the house. He had big news, too.

"Guess what! My class went on-line

today with some very famous people!" he said.

"You went on lions?" asked Andrew.

"No, not on lions," said David Michael. "We went on-*line* with our computers. That is when one computer talks to another computer."

"You mean the way you talked to Mark in Oklahoma?" I asked.

"Yup," replied David Michael. "You use a telephone line, but instead of connecting telephones, computers are connected."

"So, who did you talk to?" I asked. I wanted to find out if they really were famous people, or if David Michael was just bragging.

"First we talked to Bob Lipsky, the sports writer for the *Stoneybrook News*," David Michael replied.

"Oh," I said.

I did not care about talking to a sports writer.

"He is not the only person we talked to," continued David Michael. "We talked to

Janet Dobbins, the astronaut, too."

"You talked to Janet Dobbins?" I said.

"Yes," said David Michael, beaming. "She was very nice. She told us what it feels like to be in outer space."

I wished *I* had spoken with Janet Dobbins. Why did David Michael's class talk with her and not mine?

David Michael already knew that my class might be on *School Stars*. But I had not yet told him about Camp Outer Space. This seemed like the perfect time.

"If my class wins when we are on *School Stars*, we will get to spend a weekend at Camp Outer Space," I said. "I bet Janet Dobbins will be there. I will get to talk to her in person, not on some silly computer."

"I bet your class will not win. Not with you in it," said David Michael.

"Is that so? Well, we won against the other second-grade class today and I helped!" I replied.

"You think you are so smart. But my grades are very high now," said David Michael. "I bet my grades are higher than yours!"

"I bet you do not even know, so you should not be talking," I replied.

I stood nose to nose with David Michael.

"That is enough!" said Nannie. "Since you both want such good grades, you may have your snacks, then go to your rooms to do your homework."

"But I want to call Mark on the computer," said David Michael.

"And I want to play with Hannie," I said.

"And I want some peace and quiet," said Nannie. "So you will go to your rooms."

Boo and bullfrogs.

Studio Nine

Exciting things happened at school all week long. We took more quizzes. We practiced more stunts. And on Friday, we took a field trip to the TV studio where *School Stars* would be taped. The studio is in Stamford, Connecticut, a half-hour drive from our school.

"Thank you for coming along," Ms. Colman said to Bobby's father and Addie's mother.

They were our parent volunteers. They

have come with us on trips before. They are both very nice.

We boarded the bus and were there in no time. The TV station is in a tall, shiny building with dark glass windows. I was glad I had brought my movie star sunglasses. I put them on when we got off the bus.

"Maybe we will be discovered while we are here," I said to Hannie and Nancy. "They could make a new TV show called, 'The Three Musketeers.' "

"We will write and star in it, of course," said Nancy.

"I will direct!" I said. (I directed a movie once with my friends. They were mad at me because I was too bossy. But I learned my lesson. I think.)

"Please stay together, class," said Ms. Colman.

She led us inside. The studio was very fancy. The carpeting was gray. The walls were pale pink.

A woman wearing a gray suit and a pink blouse came out to meet us. (I wanted to ask her if she always dressed to match her office. But I did not think that would be polite.)

"Welcome to Studio Nine, home of *School Stars*. My name is Ms. Reynolds," she said. "I will show you where the show is taped. You will even see yourselves on camera today. Let's start in the green room. That is where you will wait before the show."

The green room is the room in a television studio where all the important guests wait. Remember I told you I was once in a state spelling bee? Well, the finals were on TV. That is how I know about the green room.

The room was not green. It was gray and pink like the rest of the studio. And it was crowded.

Another class of kids was in there. I thought they looked kind of young and goofy. They were giggling and falling all over each other. Our class seemed very grown-up and well behaved next to theirs.

"This is the class you will be competing against next week," said Ms. Reynolds.

This was our competition? I squeezed Hannie's hand, then Nancy's.

"I think I know who is going to win," I whispered.

The other class had finished their tour and was leaving the studio.

"See you next week!" I called.

Ms. Reynolds led us into the studio. The lights were bright and hot. I walked by a camera and waved. Next to the camera was a TV screen. Guess who was on it. My class-mates and me!

Ms. Reynolds showed us where we would stand during the show.

"Mr. Stevens, the host of the show, is sorry he could not be here today. He is looking forward to meeting you next week," she said.

By the time we left, we felt great. We

knew our way around the studio. And we had met our competition.

On the bus ride home, all we could talk about was our prize weekend at Camp Outer Space. We were going to win it. We knew it for sure!

The Challenge

The Three Musketeers were playing outside the big house after school when some kids from the neighborhood showed up. First David Michael and Linny, then Maria and Bill Korman. The Kormans live across the street. Maria is seven. Bill is nine.

"We challenge you to a game of *School Stars*!" I said.

"You got it," said Linny.

It was three of us against four of them. And Linny and Bill are both nine. But we were not worried. We were ready for them.

Maria ran home and came back with a box of Big Brain Quiz cards. The box had not even been opened yet. That is how we knew she and Bill could not have memorized the answers.

We agreed on some stunts. Then Bill pulled the first card from the box.

"For three points, tell us how many stars are on the American flag," he read.

"Ding, ding, ding!" I shouted. (We did not have bells for each player. So we just called out when we wanted to answer.)

"Karen, your answer please," said Bill.

"There are fifty stars!" I said.

"You are correct. Your team now has three points," Bill replied.

"Yea!" my friends and I shouted.

Since I answered correctly, I got to read the next question.

"For three points, which planet appears to be red?" I asked.

"Um, ding, ding!" called David Michael. "Jupiter!"

"No, I am sorry, that is incorrect," I replied. "And next time, please wait for your name to be called before answering."

David Michael stuck his tongue out at me.

It was my team's turn to answer the question. It was up to Hannie or Nancy. I hoped one of them knew that Mars is the planet that appears to be red.

Uh-oh. They did not look too sure. Finally Nancy said, "Saturn?"

I wanted to say yes because Nancy is my teammate. But I had to say, "I am sorry. That answer is incorrect. It is time for stunt number one."

The stunt was to run around two trees, do five jumping jacks, then recite the Pledge of Allegiance, all in a minute and a half.

"On your marks, get set, go!" I said.

David Michael and Nancy ran around the trees. David Michael finished a little bit ahead. They each did five jumping jacks. Then Nancy was ahead. They were shouting out the Pledge when the rest of us

BIG BRAIN
QUIZ CARDS

looked at our watches and called, "Time's up!"

David Michael stamped his foot on the ground because he had lost. He looked unhappy. By the end of *School Stars* he was furious. That is because my team won.

David Michael was not upset because we answered more questions correctly. After all, Linny and Bill, who are older, got as many answers wrong as he did. David Michael was upset because my team was better at the stunts. We had finished each one with time to spare.

As he stormed off with Linny, I heard him say, "I cannot believe they did so well at those stunts. They are only girls!"

Hannie and Nancy and I looked at each other and smiled.

"We showed him!" I said.

Blast Off!

The next time I played with Hannie and Nancy, I was back at the little house. A whole month had gone by since Ms. Colman first told my class about *School Stars.*

My friends and I had been talking about Camp Outer Space ever since we met the class we were going to compete against. We just knew we would win the Camp Outer Space prize.

"Let's pretend we are already there," said Hannie.

"Okay," said Nancy.

"Let's do this right," I added. "First we need to pack our bags."

I love packing bags. Whenever I pack a bag, it means I am going someplace exciting. Sometimes Mommy has to help me because I try to stuff in too much. But this time I was only pretend packing.

The suitcases were down in the basement, so we packed shopping bags instead. We threw in clothes and books and toys. We put in a flashlight. We even went to the kitchen and made a travel snack.

"Where are you girls going that you need so much food?" asked Mommy. We had packed every pretzel and peanut in the cupboard.

"We are practice-packing for our trip to Camp Outer Space," I replied.

"Don't forget to send me postcards while you are away," said Mommy.

"Postcards!" I said. We ran upstairs to pack some.

We took our bags out to the yard and boarded a pretend bus. We even got tied up in a traffic jam on the way.

"I hope they do not start without us," said Nancy.

The bus trip was especially bumpy. But finally we arrived. We climbed up into the tree house in my yard. We pretended that Camp Outer Space was dark. And a little scary.

"Look, I see Neptune and Pluto!" said Hannie, pointing up to the sky.

"Far out!" I replied. (I said that because Neptune and Pluto are the farthest planets from Earth.)

We put on our shiny space suits. (Mommy let us have some old tin foil she had been saving. We used it to make space collars.)

"Earth Space Station calling Musketeer Three! Are you ready for takeoff?" I said. (Musketeer Three was the name we gave our spaceship.)

"Checking instrument panel now," said Nancy. "All systems look okay."

"We are ready for takeoff," said Hannie.

"Beginning countdown," I said.

We counted down together: "Ten, nine, eight, seven, six, five, four, three, two, one . . ."

"Blast off!" we shouted. We closed our eyes and imagined ourselves shooting up into the sky.

The Three Musketeers were in orbit, waving to Earth far below.

Showing Off

"One more day to *School Stars!*" I sang to Hannie and Nancy at recess.

When we returned to the room, we had our regular math lesson and took some more quizzes. Before the bell rang, Ms. Colman gave us final instructions for our big day.

"I suggest you go home, rest, and have a nice relaxing evening. That way you will be fresh for the cameras tomorrow," said Ms. Colman.

This sounded like a good idea to me. But before I rested, I was going to have some fun. I was going to Hannie's house after school.

We rode the school bus together, then walked to the big house so I could say hello to everyone.

Daddy, Kristy, Nannie, and Emily were home. They wished us good luck and promised to tape the show.

"I will wave to you on TV!" I said.

Hannie and I were about to leave when David Michael walked in. He looked as though he had big news. Lately, he always had big news when he came home from school.

"Guess what!" he said. "My computer pal and I wrote a story on-line together and it is going to be published in the school newspaper."

Then he turned to me and said, "Second-graders hardly ever get stories in the paper."

I knew he was just showing off because I was going to be on *School Stars* and he was not.

"Congratulations!" said Daddy. "I would love to read your story."

"That is not all," said David Michael. "Here are my quizzes and an essay from school this week."

He took a stack of papers from his book bag and waved them in the air. I could see a few grades written in red. They were all 100s. There was a big, red A+ and the words "Good job!" written at the top of the essay.

Daddy looked at the papers and his face lit up. "This is terrific," he said. "David Michael, I am very proud of you."

"Big deal," I mumbled just loudly enough for David Michael to hear.

"It is a big deal," he replied. "When was the last time you got two perfect papers in one day?"

"I always get high grades and you know it," I said.

"That is enough bickering," said Daddy. "I am proud of both of you whenever you do your best."

"Some people's best is better than other people's," I said.

"Karen Brewer!" exclaimed Nannie. "If you do not have something nice to say, please do not say anything at all."

I zipped up my lips. That is because I did not have a single nice thing to say to my brother. He was making me mad. He did not have to act like a big shot just because he had a few good days at school.

"Come on, Karen," said Hannie. "We better get over to my house or my mom will start worrying."

I said good-bye to everyone except David Michael. I gave him a meanie-mo look. Then I went to Hannie's house to play. I did not have much fun, though. I kept thinking about David Michael showing off.

When I was back at the little house, I was not able to rest and relax the way Ms. Colman wanted me to. I was still too mad.

I tried thinking about *School Stars* when I got into bed. But my mind kept wandering. I was mad at David Michael and there was no room for anything else.

Welcome to
School Stars!

When I hopped out of bed the next morning, I could hardly remember what I had been so mad about the night before. All I knew was that in a few hours, I was going to be on TV.

I put on my gray jumper, gray tights, pink turtleneck, and shiny black party shoes. If Ms. Reynolds could match the studio, so could I.

After breakfast, I rode the bus to school with Nancy. Ms. Colman was already in the classroom when we arrived. Our parent volunteers, Mr. Gianelli and Mrs. Sidney, were there, too.

"Good morning, class," said Ms. Colman. "Our bus is waiting outside. So please line up and follow me."

Suddenly I felt butterflies fluttering in my stomach. Even though I had been on TV before, I felt nervous.

On the bus, Ms. Colman gave us last minute reminders about being good guests and good sports. Then we all sang the *School Stars* theme song:

School stars up in the sky.
School stars flying high.
School stars. Golden-rule stars.
Keep shining bright!

Before we knew it, we were pulling into the parking lot of Studio Nine. Ms. Reynolds greeted us and led us to the green room to meet Mr. Stevens, the host of the show.

"Welcome," said Mr. Stevens. "You look like a lively group. Is everybody ready?"

"Ready!" we replied.

"Come right this way," said Mr. Stevens.

The class we met before was already on-stage. They were seated to the right of a podium. Mr. Stevens seated us on the left. The other class looked as wimpy as the first time we saw them.

"Smile, everybody," said Mr. Stevens. "Our show is about to begin."

A woman began counting down from ten. When she got to number one, the *School Stars* theme song began to play. I wanted to sing along. But Mr. Stevens had told us to smile, not sing. So I kept quiet.

When the song was over, Mr. Stevens said, "Good morning, viewers everywhere. We have two lively teams waiting to play *School Stars*. Let's welcome Mr. Arnold's second-grade class from Hilford Elementary School and Ms. Colman's second-grade class from Stoneybrook Academy."

I heard lots of clapping and cheering in the studio. But I did not see any audience. Hmm. I guess the sounds were on tape.

"Let's get right into our game," said Mr. Stevens. "For three points, who can name a planet in our solar system that is surrounded by rings?"

Ding, ding, ding!

A kid from Mr. Arnold's class rang the bell. She was fast.

"Your answer, please," said Mr. Stevens.

"Saturn is surrounded by rings," said the girl.

"That is correct!" replied Mr. Stevens. "Your team now has three points. Here is the next question. For three points, how many times does the letter 's' appear in "Mississippi?"

Ding, ding, ding!

Guess who rang the bell. And guess who got the answer right.

"There are four esses in Mississippi," I said.

By the end of the first round, the other class was ahead five points. I was not worried, though. The class looked pretty wimpy. And the stunts were still to come.

And the Winner Is . . .

Mr. Stevens gave us a short break. When the break was over, he smiled into the camera and said, "We are now in our final round of *School Stars*. For three points, name three states in the U.S. beginning with the letter O."

It was quiet onstage for a minute. We were all thinking. Then *ding, ding, ding!* Someone from my class rang the bell. It was Natalie.

"Your answer, please," said Mr. Stevens.

"Oklahoma, Ohio, Alabama," said Natalie. "No, wait! It's not Alabama. It's um, um . . ."

Natalie looked upset.

"I am sorry. That was not the correct answer," said Mr. Stevens.

Ding, ding, ding!

A boy from Mr. Arnold's class rang the bell.

"Oklahoma, Ohio, Ontario!" he said.

"I am sorry. That is not correct," said Mr. Stevens. He tooted on a horn, then reached under the podium and pulled out a hat. Across the front it said, *Stunt-Man Stevens*.

"It is time for our first silly stunt of the show!" he said.

He pointed to three kids from Mr. Arnold's class. Then he pointed to Natalie and Ricky and me.

An assistant host ran onstage with an armload of shiny yellow wetsuits.

"You better put these on," said Stunt-Man Stevens.

I waved to Hannie and Nancy. This was

TUB 'O
Jell-O

so cool. I wondered why we needed wet-suits. I soon found out.

Two more assistants came out. Each one rolled a tub of wiggling, jiggling Jell-O onto the stage.

"It is time to jump in the Jell-O, kids," said Stunt-Man Stevens. "There are rubber grapes and rubber bananas buried in each tub. When I sound the gong, jump in the Jell-O and start picking fruit. You get one point for each piece you collect. You have sixty seconds."

A timer on the wall was ticking away. Five, four, three, two, one. *Bong, bong, bong!* Stunt-Man Stevens sounded the gong and we jumped into the Jell-O.

It was slooshy, sloshy, wiggly, and jiggly! I could not move through it very fast. Some of it went in my mouth. It was strawberry. Yum!

"I found a grape!" I cried, holding it up in the air.

"I found a banana!" called Ricky.

"I have two grapes!" called Natalie.

We were doing great. Then the gong sounded and our time was up.

When Stunt-Man Stevens announced the score, I was shocked. I was amazed. I almost fell over. Mr. Arnold's wimpy second grade won by a landslide!

"How did they do that?" I whispered to Hannie and Nancy when I got back to my place.

"They were fast," Nancy replied.

Mr. Stevens was asking another question.

"For two points, how many ounces are in two cups?" he said.

Terri answered eight. A girl from Mr. Arnold's class answered ten.

"Sixteen!" I shouted. But I was too late.

Our teams had to do another stunt. Each player had to stand in a line with a spoon and pass a raw egg to his classmate. Mr. Stevens picked Pamela, Bobby, and Addie. My team dropped their egg with a splat. Mr. Arnold's class passed the egg down the line. It hardly even wobbled.

At the end of the show, Mr. Stevens counted up the points.

"And the winner is . . . Mr. Arnold's second grade from Hilford Elementary School. Congratulations!" he said.

They won? We lost? I could hardly believe my ears.

An Excellent Prize

Mr. Arnold's class went wild cheering onstage. When they saw us looking their way, they quieted down a little. I think they did not want us to feel bad. They were pretty nice.

Ms. Colman suggested we congratulate them, so we did.

Then Mr. Stevens announced the prizes. "The first prize is a *School Stars* trophy and a weekend at Camp Outer Space," he said. He handed Mr. Arnold the trophy for his class. It was gold and shaped like a rocketship.

"We do not want Ms. Colman's class to go away empty-handed. To thank you for being part of our show, you will be receiving a classroom computer. We hope you will enjoy using it," said Mr. Stevens.

Wow! A computer! The Three Musketeers gave the thumbs-up sign. This was an excellent prize. Now I could go on-line with famous people just like David Michael did. Maybe we would get computer pals, too.

"How about a thank-you cheer for Mr. Stevens?" said Ms. Colman.

When she gave the sign, both classes shouted, "Two, four, six, eight, who do we appreciate? Stunt-Man Stevens! Stunt-Man Stevens! Hooray!"

Then we boarded the bus back to our school.

"I cannot believe Mr. Arnold's class won," said Hannie.

"They looked wimpy. But they were not.

They were great at those stunts," said Nancy.

"They sure surprised me," I replied.

"Oh, well. We tried our best. I wish we had won the trip to Camp Outer Space, though," said Nancy.

"Me, too." I said. "But, you know what? A computer is very cool."

Going On-line

A few weeks later the computer was in our room and all set up. Ms. Colman showed us exciting things such as booting up. (That means turning on the machine.) Our computer even had a modem so we could go on-line.

Thanks to David Michael I already knew that a modem lets one computer communicate with another over phone lines. And I knew that on-line had nothing to do with lions.

We learned new things every day. One morning I even went on-line with Daddy at his office. He was so surprised when he saw my message. It said:

Hi, Daddy! Guess where I am? I am at school. How are you?

We had a very nice chat. Daddy told me he was going to make meatballs and spaghetti for dinner.

In the afternoon, Ms. Colman said, "I have arranged for an on-line session next week with Edith Moss. She is an expert on endangered animals. Tomorrow we will read about species that are in danger so we can have questions ready for her," said Ms. Colman.

Then Ms. Colman looked at her watch and smiled.

"Right now, I have a surprise for you. Everyone gather round the computer and keep your eyes on the screen. We are going to be getting a call very soon."

Beep, beep. Whirr. A minute later, our computer started making on-line receiving sounds. The screen went blank, then a message appeared.

Hello, friends in Stoneybrook! How are you? Tell us something exciting!

The message was signed,

Ms. Mandel's class, New York City.

All right! We were on-line with our New York City pen pals. Now they were our computer pals, too. Ms. Colman gave each of us a chance to talk on-line.

Hi, Maxie! Did you catch me on <u>School Stars</u>? Did you see me walking around in Jell-O? It was strawberry, in case you were wondering.

Maxie wrote back that she saw the show and thought I did great even if my class did not win. We caught up on all our news.

94

Now Maxie and I could write letters, visit, *and* chat on-line.

Having a computer in the classroom was so much fun. Too bad David Michael was such a grouchy show-off. Too bad we were mad at each other. If he and I were talking, we could go on-line. We could teach each other things we learned about our computers. That would be great.

Maybe one of these days we would make up. I hoped it would not take too long.

L. GODWIN

About the Author

ANN M. MARTIN lives in New York City and loves animals, especially cats. She has two cats of her own, Gussie and Woody.

Other books by Ann M. Martin that you might enjoy are *Stage Fright*; *Me and Katie (the Pest)*; and the books in *The Baby-sitters Club* series.

Ann likes ice cream and *I Love Lucy*. And she has her own little sister, whose name is Jane.

Little Sister

Don't miss #78

KAREN'S HALF BIRTHDAY

"In two weeks, I will be seven and a half like most of the kids in my class," I told Goosie. "I will not be a seven-year-old baby anymore."

Hmm. I was getting an idea. I decided to try it out on Goosie.

"What do you think of this?" I said. "I will give myself a half birthday party. It will be just like a regular birthday party, but everything will be in half. I will serve half a birthday cake. I will invite half the kids in my class. I will ask each guest to bring half a present."

I could tell Goosie thought this was an excellent idea.

"What did you say? You want me to bring you a whole piece of birthday cake? I am sorry. Half pieces, only," I said.